EDGE BOOKS

BLOODIEST BATTLES

THE WORLD COLLIDES

THE BATTLE OF GALLIPOLI

BY TERRI DOUGHERTY

CONSULTANT:
Tim Solie
Adjunct Professor of History
Minnesota State University, Mankato

Capstone
press®
Mankato, Minnesota

Edge Books are published by Capstone Press,
151 Good Counsel Drive, P.O. Box 669, Mankato, Minnesota 56002.
www.capstonepress.com

Library of Congress Cataloging-in-Publication Data
Dougherty, Terri.
    The world collides : the Battle of Gallipoli / by Terri Dougherty.
    p. cm. — (Edge books. Bloodiest battles)
    Includes bibliographical references and index.
    Summary: "Describes events before, during, and after the Battle of
Gallipoli, including key players, weapons, and battle tactics" — Provided
by publisher.
    ISBN-13: 978-1-4296-2298-1 (hardcover)
    ISBN-10: 1-4296-2298-9 (hardcover)
    1. World War, 1914–1918 — Campaigns — Turkey — Gallipoli
Peninsula — Juvenile literature. I. Title. II. Series.
D568.3.D68 2009
940.4'26 — dc22
                                     2008025457

Editorial Credits

Aaron Sautter, editor; Bob Lentz, set designer; Kim Brown,
    book designer/illustrator; Jo Miller, photo researcher

Photo Credits

Alamy/Dominic Whiting, 29; Mary Evans Picture Library, 12;
    The Print Collector, 8 (top left)
Corbis/Bettmann, 4, 20–21, 24, 26
Getty Images Inc./Edward Gooch, 7 (bottom right); Hulton Archive,
    cover (foreground), 7 (bottom left), 23; Imagno, 7 (top left); Keystone,
    7 (top right); Popperfoto, 16; Three Lions, 10; Time Life Pictures/
    Mansell, 8 (top right); Time Life Pictures/National Archives, 13
Library of Congress/Harris & Ewing, 8 (bottom)
Newscom, cover (background)

1 2 3 4 5 6   14 13 12 11 10 09

TABLE OF CONTENTS

CHAPTER 1

A WORLD AT WAR

Allied battleships pounded the Turkish defenses to begin the Battle of Gallipoli.

As the sun rose on April 25, 1915, the boom of navy guns echoed through the air. Allied soldiers made their way toward Gallipoli's shore. Turkish soldiers fired at the Allied troops from a high ridge. Bullets whizzed toward transport ships carrying soldiers to the beaches. By the end of the day, the water was red with blood.

The Allies wanted to take the Gallipoli **Peninsula** out of Turkish control. This would prove to be a deadly task. The Battle of Gallipoli lasted for nine months. Allied soldiers fought from **trenches** and ravines while Turkish forces rained down bullets from above.

peninsula — a piece of land that is surrounded by water on three sides

trench — a long, narrow ditch

5

> WORLD WAR I BEGINS

FACT: On June 28, 1914, Archduke Franz Ferdinand of Austria was killed. The other leaders of Austria-Hungary believed Serbia was responsible. They declared war on Serbia on July 28, 1914, beginning World War I.

The Central Powers

The first shots at Gallipoli rang out less than a year after World War I (1914–1918) began. Much of the fighting during the war took place in France and Russia. However, Turkey was also involved in the war. The Battle of Gallipoli was fought in northwestern Turkey near the Black Sea.

In World War I, Turkey was part of the Ottoman Empire. The Ottoman Empire agreed to help Austria-Hungary and Germany during the war. Together these countries formed an **alliance** called the **Central powers**. The countries agreed to help each other in times of war so they could hold on to their power.

alliance — an agreement between groups to work together

Central powers — a group of countries that fought the Allied Powers in World War I

Sultan Mehmed V, Ottoman Empire

Emperor Franz Josef I, Austria-Hungary

Kaiser Wilhelm II, Germany

Archduke Franz Ferdinand, Austria

Prime Minister Herbert Henry Asquith, Great Britain

Czar Nicholas II, Russia

President Woodrow Wilson, United States

8

The Allied Powers

Before World War I, the map of Europe looked very different than it does today. Germany and Austria-Hungary controlled most of central Europe. The Ottoman Empire controlled much of eastern Europe and the Middle East. Together, the Central powers were very strong. But they wanted to gain even more territory.

A large group of countries called the **Allied powers** opposed the Central powers. The Allied nations were led by Great Britain, France, and Russia. The Allies didn't want the Central powers to completely control Europe. They began fighting the Central powers in August 1914. The United States joined the Allies in 1917.

Allied powers — a group of countries that fought the Central Powers in World War I

CHAPTER 2

STUCK IN THE TRENCHES

Fighting from the trenches
was dirty and dangerous.

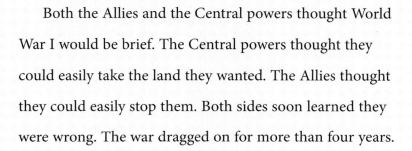

Both the Allies and the Central powers thought World War I would be brief. The Central powers thought they could easily take the land they wanted. The Allies thought they could easily stop them. Both sides soon learned they were wrong. The war dragged on for more than four years.

Central Powers' Strategy

Germany had a strong army. Its soldiers were the best-trained force in Europe. Germany planned to first defeat France. Then it planned to help Austria-Hungary fight against Russia.

In 1914, the Germans marched across Belgium toward Paris, France. The Allies were ready for them. They stopped Germany's troops from advancing. When the Germans could go no farther, they dug in. They built a trench line to prevent Allied forces from taking back the lands Germany controlled.

> DISEASE IN THE TRENCHES

FACT:

Bullets and bombs weren't the only dangers soldiers faced in the war. Filthy conditions in the trenches allowed deadly diseases to spread. Tens of thousands of soldiers died from diseases.

Allies' Strategy

The Central powers had well-trained and organized armies. But the Allies had the advantage of more manpower. This advantage helped more as the war went on.

Like Germany, the Allies also built trenches at the battlefront. Soldiers stayed in trenches for protection from enemy fire. When it was time for battle, they burst out of the trenches while firing their rifles. They also used bayonets. These sharp blades were attached to the ends of soldiers' rifles. Soldiers used bayonets in hand-to-hand combat with the enemy.

Soldiers had a name for charging out of a trench. They called it "going over the top."

> NEW WEAPONS IN WORLD WAR I

Many new ways of fighting battles began in World War I. Tanks were used in war for the first time. These huge machines were armed with powerful guns. But sometimes they were too slow and heavy. They often got stuck in the mud.

Airplanes were also new weapons. Pilots often fought their enemies in air battles called dogfights. The most famous World War I pilot was Manfred von Richthofen. Nicknamed the "Red Baron," this German ace won nearly 80 dogfights during the war.

One of the newest and deadliest weapons was poison gas. It had a horrible effect on soldiers' bodies. Chlorine gas caused soldiers to choke. Yellow-brown mustard gas led to serious blisters — both inside and outside the body. The gas burned and blinded soldiers. It usually caused serious lung damage. Soldiers wore gas masks to protect themselves, but the masks didn't always work well.

Stalemate and a New Plan

Trench warfare both helped and hurt the war effort on both sides. Trench lines ran across Europe. Allied trenches kept Germany from moving into Allied territory. But the German trenches also kept the Allies from moving farther into Europe. Neither side could gain any ground.

Many of the Allied forces fought on the western front in France. Russia fought for the Allies in the east. In 1915, Russia needed more troops and supplies. The Allies had to figure out how to help Russia.

The Allies decided to go around the trench line. They thought the best way would be to go through the Dardanelles **strait** in Turkey. If they could get into the Black Sea, they could send Russia the support it needed. But to succeed, the Allies first had to capture the Gallipoli Peninsula.

The Allies also wanted to control Constantinople, which was the capital of the Ottoman Empire. The Allies thought controlling Gallipoli and Constantinople would weaken the Central Powers. They hoped it would help bring a quick end to the war.

strait — a narrow strip of water that connects two larger bodies of water

> SUPPORTING RUSSIA

LOCATION: Gallipoli Peninsula, Turkey

DATE: March 1915

OBJECTIVE: Send troops and supplies to Russia

MAP

N

ATLANTIC
OCEAN

= WESTERN TRENCH LINE
= EASTERN FRONT
= ALLIES' PLANNED ROUTE
= ALLIED POWERS
= CENTRAL POWERS
= NEUTRAL COUNTRIES
= CAPITAL CITY

NORWAY

SWEDEN

DENMARK

[BALTIC SEA]

[NORTH SEA]

NETHERLANDS

GERMANY

GREAT
BRITAIN

RUSSIA

FRANCE

SWITZERLAND

AUSTRIA-HUNGARY

SPAIN

ITALY

[BLACK SEA]

CONSTANTINOPLE

GALLIPOLI
PENINSULA

GREECE

TURKEY
(OTTOMAN EMPIRE)

[MEDITERRANEAN SEA]

AFRICA

CHAPTER 3

A COSTLY BATTLE

Allied battleships used huge guns to fire at the Turkish defenses on shore.

On March 18, 1915, a huge fleet of Allied ships prepared to fight through the Dardanelles strait. Their engines roared as they headed into battle.

A Failed Naval Attack

Gunfire boomed as the ships neared the strait. The *Queen Elizabeth* and other battleships began blasting their big guns. They fired at the Turkish forts on the high ridges overlooking the sea.

As the ships advanced, explosions rocked the water. The strait was peppered with mines. Minesweepers tried to clear the channel. But they came under heavy fire and had to turn back. The larger ships tried to get through, but several were damaged by mine blasts and heavy gunfire.

By 2:00 in the afternoon, the Allies were in trouble. The French ship *Bouvet* hit a line of mines and quickly sank. More than 600 sailors drowned. The battleship *Irresistible* was also destroyed. The Allied ships couldn't get past the Turkish defenses. They were forced to turn back.

Taking the Beaches

The naval **offensive** had failed. However, the Allies still wanted to control Gallipoli. They decided to send in land forces to take out the Turkish guns. The minesweepers would then be able to clear the channel for the larger ships.

On April 25, 1915, hundreds of ships again made their way toward Gallipoli. They carried tens of thousands of soldiers who would land at several beaches. Several battleships would hammer the enemy lines so the soldiers could make it to shore.

But the Turkish Army was prepared to fight. Turkish officer Mustafa Kemal wanted to stop the Allies from advancing. He had his troops dig trenches above the beaches. They hid in the trenches and waited for the Allies' attack.

The guns of the Allied battleships thundered as the troops headed toward shore. The troops didn't know what they would find when they got there. Turkish bullets hailed down on them as they tried to land. Many soldiers died before they even reached the shore.

offensive — a military attack

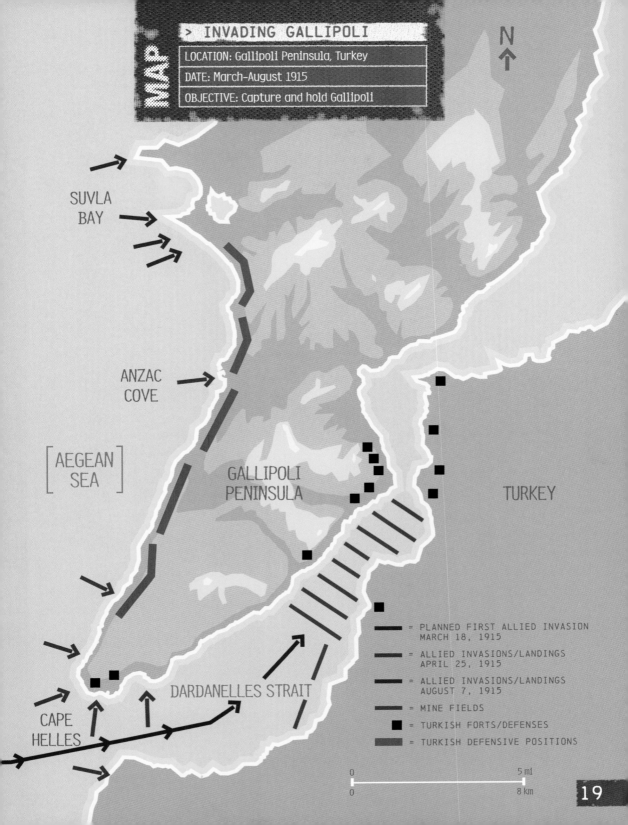

> INVADING GALLIPOLI

LOCATION: Gallipoli Peninsula, Turkey

DATE: March-August 1915

OBJECTIVE: Capture and hold Gallipoli

MAP

N

SUVLA
BAY

ANZAC
COVE

[AEGEAN
SEA]

GALLIPOLI
PENINSULA

TURKEY

DARDANELLES STRAIT

CAPE
HELLES

= PLANNED FIRST ALLIED INVASION
MARCH 18, 1915

= ALLIED INVASIONS/LANDINGS
APRIL 25, 1915

= ALLIED INVASIONS/LANDINGS
AUGUST 7, 1915

= MINE FIELDS

■ = TURKISH FORTS/DEFENSES

= TURKISH DEFENSIVE POSITIONS

0   5 ml

0   8 km

Disorder and Dismay

Many soldiers who did make it to shore didn't know where to go. Much of the land was rocky and steep. Beaches were covered with thick brush and barbed wire. The men had to fight through the barriers while Turkish soldiers shot at them.

> ANZAC FORCES

FACT:

Many of the troops at Gallipoli came from Australia and New Zealand. They were called ANZAC forces. ANZAC stood for Australia and New Zealand Army Corps.

The Allied soldiers tried to get to high ground but couldn't find a good path. Groups got separated as they followed different paths. Many paths led to dead ends. Meanwhile, Turkish soldiers kept shooting at the Allies from above.

The rattle of gunfire and the groans of wounded soldiers filled the air. By evening, the beaches were filled with dead bodies. The sand was stained red with blood.

Thousands of ANZAC forces landed at ANZAC Cove and Suvla Bay.

Withdrawal

In spite of the Allies' heavy losses, some soldiers survived the invasion. They began to work their way inland. But they soon came to a standstill. The Turkish Army had good protection in their deep trenches. The Allies couldn't make it past the Turkish defenses.

The Allies dug in too. They built their own trenches and shelters. They then began launching more attacks. In the summer of 1915, the Allies tried several times to get through the Turkish defenses. But they couldn't advance. They suffered many **casualties**.

The Allied soldiers suffered from more than bullet wounds. Sometimes they ran low on water, food, and bullets. Soldiers in the trenches also suffered from disease and bad weather. The trenches filled with water when large storms came. Soldiers sometimes drowned in the trenches. The storms also ruined many buildings and shelters.

The Allies struggled to make it through autumn. By early winter, they knew they couldn't hold on any longer. They decided to retreat from Gallipoli. The Allies began withdrawing troops on December 10, 1915. By January 9, 1916, the Allied troops had completely left Gallipoli. The bold offensive was over.

casualty — a soldier who is missing, captured, injured, or killed in battle

Life in the trenches was a miserable experience.

CHAPTER 4

AN UNEASY PEACE

The United States added many troops to the war effort beginning in 1917.

LEARN ABOUT

> END OF WORLD WAR I
> WAR CASUALTIES
> AFTER THE WAR

The Allies' attempt to take Gallipoli had failed. They couldn't get through the Dardanelles strait to help Russia. Meanwhile, the Central powers remained strong.

The United States Enters the War

World War I raged on in Europe. On the western front, Allied forces continued fighting Germany in France. Russia battled both the Austro-Hungarian and Turkish armies in the east.

The Allies made little progress. By 1917, the Central powers controlled Poland, Romania, and Serbia. They also held Belgium and part of France.

In April 1917, the United States entered the war. German submarines were sinking U.S. merchant ships near Great Britain. The United States wanted to stop Germany's attacks on ships at sea. U.S. leaders also wanted to support countries working for **democracy** in Europe. The United States gave the Allies more troops and military supplies.

democracy — a form of government in which the citizens can choose their leaders

25

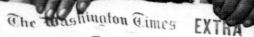

The Washington Times EXTRA

GERMANY SURRENDERS

LONDON—Germany has agreed to the armistice terms laid down
by the allies. It is understood the terms are virtually the same as those
which were signed by Austria providing for occupation of a large number
of towns by the allies, demobilization of the enemy armies and turning

The Washington Times FINAL EDITION

WAR IS OVER

Enemy Stripped of Power By Terms of Agreement

FIGHTING At 2 P. M. Paris Time STOPPED
At 9 A. M. Our Time

The war is over.

Germany and the allies signed an armistice at 11 o'clock today,
hostilities ceasing three hours later.

As Marshal Foch's terms are known to include provisions which will
prevent resumption of hostilities the greatest war of all time
to an end. Germany by the terms of the armistice
power to reopen the war.

At the time the document was signed the
smashing forward on a 150 mile front, from the
tearing the German defenses to pieces and driv
rout. The Americans took Sedan this mor
made at all points on the battle front.

Before the terms were submitted to Germany,
Marshal Foch and Admiral Wemyss, as military and
under a flag of truce.

While actual peace was thus being conclude
revolution at home. A revolt of sai
Holstein and several large cities were

FLASH WITH THE NEWS

When Germany surrendered, people around
the world celebrated the end of the war.

Allied Victory

In early 1918, Germany launched a strong offensive. Its leaders wanted to capture Paris, France. But the Allies were able to push back the Germans. That summer, the Allies finally broke through Germany's trench line. Germany was forced to retreat.

Soon all the Central powers began to weaken. Russia was too strong for the Turkish Army. Austria-Hungary lost a large battle against Italy. And in Germany, food and supplies began to run low.

The Central powers soon realized they couldn't win the war. The Ottoman Empire agreed to stop fighting on October 30, 1918. On November 3, Austria-Hungary signed a peace treaty. Germany surrendered on November 11. World War I had come to an end.

The Costs of War

The Battle of Gallipoli was costly for both sides. By the time the Allies withdrew, at least 252,000 Allied soldiers had been killed or wounded. Meanwhile, the Turkish forces suffered about 300,000 casualties.

The battle was costly in other ways too. Because the Allies lost at Gallipoli, World War I dragged on for three more years. The Allies suffered more than 19 million casualties during the war. The Central powers had more than 12 million casualties. Much of Europe was destroyed. People struggled to find food and a safe place to live.

After the war, the Allies forced Germany to pay for the damage it had done. This caused resentment in Germany. Germany's leaders didn't feel they should have to pay. And some still wanted to conquer Europe. Within 20 years, World War II erupted to tear Europe apart all over again.

> GALLIPOLI TODAY

FACT:

In 1980, the Gallipoli area was turned into a national park. Gallipoli Peninsula Peace Park covers 127 square miles (329 square kilometers).

Many monuments at Gallipoli Peninsula Peace Park honor the men who fought and died at Gallipoli.

GLOSSARY

alliance (uh-LY-uhnts) — an agreement between groups to work together

Allied powers (AL-lyd PAU-uhrs) — a group of countries that fought the Central powers in World War I; the Allies included the United States, England, France, Russia, and Italy.

casualty (KAZH-oo-uhl-tee) — a soldier who is missing, captured, injured, or killed in battle

Central powers (SEN-truhl PAU-uhrs) — a group of countries that fought the Allied powers in World War I; the Central powers included Germany, Turkey, and Austria-Hungary.

democracy (di-MAH-kruh-see) — a form of government in which people can choose their leaders

offensive (uh-FEN-siv) — a military attack

peninsula (puh-NIN-suh-luh) — a piece of land that is surrounded by water on three sides

strait (STRAYT) — a narrow strip of water that connects two larger bodies of water

trench (TRENCH) — a long, narrow ditch; soldiers fight in trenches during wars.

READ MORE

Adams, Simon. *World War I.* DK Eyewitness Books.
New York: DK, 2007.

Hamilton, John. *Battles of World War I.* World War I.
Edina, Minn.: Abdo, 2004.

Hibbert, Adam. *In the Trenches in World War I.*
On the Front Line. Chicago: Raintree, 2006.

INTERNET SITES

FactHound offers a safe, fun way to find
educator-approved Internet sites related
to this book.

Here's what to do:
1. Visit www.facthound.com
2. Choose your grade level.
3. Begin your seach.

This book's ID number is 9781429622981.

FactHound will fetch the best sites for you!

INDEX